The Story of H. M. Stanley

GET ALL OF THE 'HISTORY SHAPERS' BOOKS
The Story of...

David Livingstone	Robert Bruce	Chalmers of New
H. M. Stanley	General Gordon	Guinea
Abraham Lincoln	Lord Clive	Bishop Patteson
Sir Francis Drake	Captain Cook	Joan of Arc
Sir Walter Raleigh	Nelson	Napoleon
Columbus	Lord Roberts	Cromwell

PLEASE NOTE

In this series, you will read about historical figures who displayed courage, bravery, self-sacrifice, and many other admirable traits. Their stories remind us that many people in history took bold actions and made tough choices. Yet, even those who achieved great things sometimes held ideas or pursued goals that were not beneficial to every-one. History is full of complex individuals—parts of their lives inspire us to be brave and stand up for what is right, while other parts remind us to consider the unintended consequences of our actions.

As you explore these biographies, we invite you to reflect on the qualities that enabled these figures to achieve greatness and the lessons we can learn from their mistakes. Maybe you too can become a History Shaper—someone who learns from the past and helps to make our world a better place for everyone.

This edition published 2025
by Living Book Press

ISBN: 978-1-76153-552-9 (hardcover)
         978-1-76153-556-7 (softcover)

First published in 1906.

A catalogue record for this book is available from the National Library of Australia

THE STORY OF
H. M. STANLEY

by

VAUTIER GOLDING

LIVING BOOK
PRESS

Contents

Early Years

The good folk of Denbigh, in North Wales, proudly claim their town to be the birthplace of the great explorer, Sir H. M. Stanley. Close by the ruin of its old Castle, they point out the little Welsh cottage where his life began; and thus they tell the story of his childhood before he left his country and changed his name.

He was born in 1841, and baptized in Tremeirchon Church as John Rowlands, which is the English way of writing the Welsh name Rollant. His father, John Rollant, a farmer's son, died when the wee child was only two years old; and his mother, who afterwards became Mrs. Jones, left him to the care of a nurse.

From that time a good and kindly woman, Mrs. Price, was a second mother to the child, and she brought him up with her own children happily enough. Her husband had charge of the Denbigh bowling-green; and while he worked at the well-kept lawn, his sturdy little foster-son ran about all day in the open air. Every one tried as much as possible to be kind to him, and the simple and homely peasant life made him grow up hardy, active, and strong.

When at length he was old enough to leave his new home, he was sent to a boarding-school at St. Asaph.

His foster-brother, Richard Price, carried the little fellow there on his shoulders, while a former nurse, Harriet Jones, went part of the way as an escort. St. Asaph was farther than John had ever yet been, and the way there must have seemed a long and strange pilgrimage to his childish mind. No doubt in after years, when he made his own toilsome way through prairie, forest, and desert, he gratefully remembered the kind folk who tried to make his first journey as easy and happy as could be.

On reaching the school, Richard Price handed over his charge and said good-bye, and John Rowlands was left to make his own way in his new surroundings. It was a severe change to come from the special love and care of his cottage home, and then to find himself just one in a crowd of boys who did not mind in the least whether he was happy or not. John, however, soon learnt how to look after himself. He was ready and keen in his work, and his pluck and vigour made him a leader among his schoolfellows. On the whole, his life at St. Asaph seems to have been a happy one, though his quick temper and masterful ways often made trouble for him.

After ten years at St. Asaph John went, at the age of sixteen, to be a pupil teacher under his cousin, who kept the National School at Mold. This arrangement, however, was not a success. The cousin appears to have been ill-natured and spiteful, and he tried in a mean way to put upon John more than his fair share of work. The boy's temper rebelled against such treatment, and there was a quarrel, which John ended by walking out of the house to fight his own way in the world.

To be alone on the highway, without a home, without a friend, and with only a few pence in his pocket, was a grim and serious plight for a lad of sixteen. John Rowlands, however, does not seem to have had any trouble at all in making up his mind what next to do, for he at once took the road to Liverpool. He had heard and read of young emigrants who had gone, poor and unknown, to America, and had come back rich and famous; and he determined to see if he could not do the same.

It was a long and weary tramp; and, at the end of it, there was no hope of a warm welcome, a good meal, and a comfortable bed. The great town of Liverpool, too, was large enough to swallow a hundred Denbighs; and its long streets of large buildings struck a cold and cheerless gloom into the heart of the lonely outcast. He asked his way through the town to the docks; and there he wandered about and watched the shipping at the wharves and in the Mersey tideway, till hunger and fatigue drove him back into the streets. Here a few pence bought him all the food he could afford; and then, when the dead of night made all things quiet, he stole up a side alley and slept in the shadow of a deep doorway.

Next morning he again went down to the docks, and found a trading ship about to start on her return voyage to New Orleans, with a number of emigrants on board. It was, of course, quite out of the question for John to pay his fare as an emigrant, and he wistfully watched the forlorn and homesick exiles troop over the gangway to their cramped and comfortless quarters on the lower deck. One or two of them were carrying in a single bundle all they had in the world, and John felt that even these were better off than himself. Then an idea struck him, and he asked some of the sailors if any more hands were wanted for the ship's crew. They took him to the captain, who liked the look of him, and said he might come on board as a cabin-boy and give work instead of money for his passage to America.

John thought himself in luck's way, though at first he could hardly believe it true. Soon, however, the ship was cast loose and hauled off the quay; then her bows slowly swung round to seaward, and she moved down the tideway, across the Mersey bar, and out to the open sea. In a few hours John saw the blue hills of his native land sink out of sight in the distance, and then he began to feel that he had lost a home.

The ship pitched and rolled as she plunged over the waves; and John, who was ordered here there and every-where to do all kinds of drudgery, found it hard to keep his feet. But, however he felt, his work had to be done; and, though he often wished himself ashore, he struggled pluckily on. In reality he was better off than the emigrants. His work kept his mind off his own woes; and thus he soon found his "sea-legs," while many of the others lay groaning about the deck.

As the voyage wore on he became more used to the new life, and his work seemed easier. He was a quick and clever lad; and, by the time the ship was off the mouth of the Mississippi, he had become quite a handy sailor. Here they were taken in tow by a steam tug, which hauled them a hundred miles upstream, among the twists and turns and mudbanks of this most dangerous river. Sometimes they would be heading due north, and then in a few minutes they would come round a bend and go straight to the southward. The deep water was now on one side of the stream, now on the other. The mudbanks, too, were always changing and shifting, so that the least mistake of the pilot might run them aground. The river ran through a land of plains and forests so vast that John's little homeland valley might easily be lost in them. It was indeed a new world to him; and among other strange sights, he now for the first time saw negroes at work in the plantations, driven by white men with whips.

At New Orleans, John said good-bye to his shipmates and went ashore to seek his fortune. He was not long in finding work as a clerk in a merchant's office, and he soon showed that he was well worth his place. His employer, whose name was Stanley, had no children of his own; and he took such a fancy to John that he adopted him as his son. John Rowlands now changed his name to Henry Morton Stanley, and was looked upon as heir to his new father's fortune.

But the merchant died without making his will; and his

relations, who divided his property among themselves, turned their backs upon his adopted son. Thus young Stanley, as John Rowlands must now be called, was once more left to make his own way.

Just at this time a civil war broke out in America. The Northern States were determined to unite together and to put down slavery in their land. The Southern States wanted to manage their own affairs and to keep their slaves. Young Stanley, who had grown accustomed to see human beings driven to labour like cattle under the whip, fought on the side of the South.

He served in the ranks of General Johnstone's army till its defeat at Pittsburg in 1862, when he was taken prisoner with many of his comrades. While the convoy of captives filed past the bend of a river, Stanley suddenly broke away, dashed down the bank and plunged into the water. Shot after shot from the escort splashed the water in his face, but he swam across and escaped into cover unharmed. Then he made his way to the sea and worked for his passage home to North Wales.

After staying awhile with his mother, he went as a clerk under an uncle in Liverpool. But his roving spirit soon grew weary of office work, and once more he worked his passage over to New York. Here, he enlisted as a seaman in the navy of the Northern States, and was soon fighting against his former friends. In one month he was made clerk to the flagship *Ticonderoga*, and in four months he became the admiral's secretary.

One day he swam under fire to fix a rope to a ship which had been deserted by the enemy, and for this he was made an ensign. Thus when peace was made he returned to Wales as a naval officer, and once more saw his mother and friends. Once more too, but for the last time, he signed his name as "John Rowlands" in the visitors' book at Denbigh Castle, showing that he had not forgotten his old home. He also remembered his schooldays, and gave all the boys at St. Asaph's a generous treat.

Not long after this he left the United States navy, and in a short while became a war correspondent to the *New York Herald*. He was sent to Abyssinia with the British force under Napier; and he managed to send news of the victory at Magdala to the American papers a whole day before the battle was reported in London.

Stanley was now nearly thirty years old; but though his life had been spent in hard work and plucky adventure, it was still rather changeful and aimless. Soon, however, he was to find a brave and unselfish hero, whose nobler spirit laid hold of Stanley's nature and drew him to the work that brought him honour and greatness.

The Search for Livingstone

About the end of the year 1870 all the world was wondering what had become of the famous explorer Dr. Livingstone. The people of America, who had just done away with slavery in their own land, took a particular interest in this great man's work against the slave trade in Africa, whence their own supply of slaves had come. As no one had heard of him for two years, many began to think he must either be dead or in great distress from sickness and want of supplies. Stanley had often talked over the chances of finding him, and thought it quite possible. White men were so scarce in Africa that it was easy to trace them by hearsay from the natives. The main difficulty lay in the dangers and hardships of the journey, and in the trouble of finding honest and faithful bearers.

At this time James Gordon Bennett, of the *New York Herald*, telegraphed for Stanley to meet him in Paris; and in a very short while it was arranged that an attempt should be made to find Livingstone. Stanley was first sent on a wonderful tour through Persia to Bombay, and thence to Zanzibar on the east coast of Africa, with orders to spare no expense in the search. He arrived at Zanzibar early in January 1871, and immediately began to get together the men and materials for the expedition. He soon engaged two white sailors, Farquhar and Shaw, and he was also lucky enough to find six of the faithful blacks who had been with Captain Speke at the head-waters of the Nile. These men said they would "go anywhere with one of Speke's brothers"; and their leader, called Bombay, quickly found eighteen more to make up an armed escort for the caravan.

The natives of Central Africa did not understand the use of money; and therefore, in order to buy food for his men, Stanley had to take with him many coils of brass wire, many pounds of beads, and hundreds of yards of calico and cloth. These, with the camp stores and baggage, and also with two boats, twenty donkeys, two horses and some goats, were all collected together by the end of the month and landed at Bagamoyo on the mainland. Here Stanley expected to get bearers to carry his supplies, but now his troubles began. One Arab promised faithfully to send him all the men he wanted, but after waiting fifteen days Stanley found out that the rascal had not the least intention of keeping his word. Stanley was helpless to find them himself and was almost in despair, when he heard of a young Arab who was to be trusted. His new friend soon collected about 160 bearers; and, acting on his advice, Stanley sent off his company in five small caravans with spaces of a few days between them.

At last on March 21, after spending six weeks at Bagamoyo, Stanley and Shaw with all the animals started in the last and largest caravan. On reaching the river Kingani the men and stores were ferried across in native canoes, while the animals swam over with a rope round their necks to guide them towards the landing on the opposite bank. The river was full of hippopotami, and often one of them would thrust his massive head above water, and blow a cloud of spray from his nostrils; then, after a puzzled look at the kicking and plunging donkeys, he would take a deep breath and dive again out of sight.

After leaving Kingani the heat grew intense, and the flies of many kinds became a plague. The men suffered much from these torments, but the poor animals, who could not protect themselves, were bitten till the blood dropped from their coats. The deadly tsetse-fly was among them, and soon one of Stanley's horses died, and was buried outside the camp. Next day the native chief of the district demanded a fine, because the dead horse had been put in his soil without his leave. Stanley refused to pay the fine, but offered to dig the horse up again and to make the ground as it had been before. The chief now asked to be friends, for he saw that his trick would not get him any cloth or beads, and so the matter ended. A few hours later Stanley's other horse died too, and there was no trouble about its burial.

Near Msuwa the caravan had to pass through ten miles of jungle, so thick that the track was in places like a small tunnel, with roof and sides lined with sharp and crooked thorns of all sizes. The men could only pass in single file, and they went crouching along to save both themselves and their packs from being cut and torn by the cruel spikes overhead. About this time a bearer, named Khamisi, deserted and slipped off into the jungle with his pack. As soon as he was missed two of the escort were sent to track him down. They followed his trail into a village, and found him tied to a tree in terror of his life from the natives, who were just making ready to kill him. On seeing the rifles of the two men, the natives released Khamisi and gave up his goods, and he was taken back to the caravan. Most people would have thought his narrow escape from death to be punishment enough; but Stanley, who was harsh and often cruel to his men, had him flogged with a donkey-whip.

On nearing Simbamwenni Stanley met an Arab trader, who told him that Livingstone had been at Ujiji nearly two years ago on his way to Manyema; this showed how slowly news travelled in the country. Still it was something to know that Livingstone was at that time alive and well enough to travel.

A few days later Stanley lost his cook, a black man called Bunder Salaam, who, for the fifth time, was caught helping himself to his master's private store of food. He had been forgiven four times, but now his hands were tied, and Stanley ordered Shaw to flog him with a whip. In addition to this, but intending only to frighten him, Stanley gave orders that the cook, with his donkey and baggage, should be turned out of camp, and be left to take his chance of reaching home alive. But as soon as the poor man's hands were loosed, he dashed away at full speed, and nothing could call him back. Stanley was now very sorry for what he had done, and he had the donkey tied to a tree, hoping that the cook would return and overtake the caravan.

They then went forward, but mile after mile was passed without a sign of the missing man. Stanley began to grow anxious, and sent men back to look for him. These men found that the donkey had been stolen by some natives, whom they also suspected of murdering the man. But though the donkey was afterwards recovered, they could find no trace of Bunder Salaam.

The rainy season had now broken upon them, but, luckily for them, it lasted only three weeks instead of the usual six. The valley of the Makata River lay before them, and the torrents of African rain had turned it into swamp and flood for a stretch of thirty miles. For two days they struggled through mire and marsh, or splashed through water till they were nearly worn out. Next day from the top of a mound they saw before them five miles of unbroken flood, reaching to the mountain range which flanked the valley. It was like a large lake, with trees, bushes and clumps of grass growing here and there in the water.

The bearers now began to throw down their burdens, and said the water was too deep; but Stanley lashed some of them into the flood with his whip, and the rest soon followed. It was terrible work plunging onward, often up to the shoulders, with burdens on their heads; cutting and tearing their feet on stones and thorns, as they groped for a footing beneath the muddy water, expecting every moment to sink out of their depth. At last the struggle was over, and they reached high ground exhausted but happy. It was the worst bit of their journey, and it left its mark upon all; for after their soaking and fatigue, fever broke out among the men, and the animals began to die off one by one.

They now crossed the beautiful slopes of the Usagara Mountains to the valley of the river Mokondokwa; and at a village, called Kiora, they came up with the third caravan. Farquhar, its leader, had been wasting the cloth and beads in feasting himself and his men, and was now lying dangerously ill in a hut. Stanley made the two caravans into one, and, on May 11, pushed forward across a stretch of wilderness to Lake Ugombo. For five days they went over bare hills and dry plains, covered only with cactus, aloes, coarse grass, thorn scrub, and dwarf trees. The lake itself seemed the haunt of hundreds of wild creatures. The marsh along its shore was everywhere marked with the spoor of hippopotamus, buffalo, zebra, giraffe, kudu, and antelope. All kinds of waterfowl fluttered in the reeds and flew over its surface, while doves cooed in the trees, and guinea-fowl screeched in the cover.

Not long after leaving the lake another man, Jako, deserted, and two days were lost in finding him. He was, tracked to a hut, where the natives had made him a prisoner, and asked a reward for his capture. Stanley gave them a gift, and chained Jako with the other runaways like a gang of slaves; and then the caravan moved on to Mpwapwa.

The hillside here was beautiful and bracing and food was in plenty, and Stanley therefore decided to have a three days' rest. In spite of its many delights there were two great drawbacks to comfort in the place, for the earwigs and white ants were a plague. The earwigs invaded Stanley's tent by hundreds; they covered his baggage and camped in his hammock by the dozen; they crawled over his food, into his pockets and boots, under his clothes, and about his face. In short, they seemed to think it their duty to examine anxiously not only all he possessed, but every square inch of each thing. The white ants came in battalions, and the amount of matting, cloth, and leather that they could eat, even in an hour, was almost beyond belief.

Farquhar was now too ill to travel, and was left to the care of a friendly chief, with Jako for a nurse. The donkeys were reduced to ten, and four of these were unfit for loads; but Stanley was lucky enough to find twelve new bearers. He now joined two Arab caravans, and together they crossed the Marenga wilderness, where they were without water for thirty-six hours, and came into the Ugogo country.

Here they had to pay tax to every chief whose borders they passed. The Sultan of Mvumi was a most grasping man. Stanley sent him a present of six pieces of cloth, and a messenger at once came back to demand forty more. Stanley chafed at this greed, but was forced to pay. Six more were then demanded and paid. Still another message came, and, after paying three more pieces, Stanley was allowed to go onward.

Leaving Mvumi on May 27, after losing five donkeys in one night, they made their way to Matambaru; and then passed through another stretch of dense jungle in single file by a dark and narrow path. Here a bearer sank down with sickness and fatigue, and his caravan passed on and left him. He died before the last caravan had gone by, and some of them stopped to bury him.

At Nyambwa the natives had never seen a white man, and they crowded round Stanley in such numbers that they blocked the way. Stanley at last caught one of them by the neck and thrashed him; and though the others mobbed him for a long way with hoots and curses, they kept out of the way of his whip.

Soon after this they reached the Kiti defile, and crossed the range of hills to Tura by a steep and rugged path. On the way another bearer dropped out of the ranks, and was left to die. At Shiza, Stanley had a bullock killed for a farewell feast; and then, on June 23, they marched into Unyanyembe, 185 days after leaving Bagamoyo. Stanley now took up his quarters at Kwihara, one mile from the chief Arab town Tabora, and he began to prepare for the march to Ujiji.

Livingstone Found at Ujiji

Stanley's plans for the march to Ujiji were upset by an attack of fever so bad that for ten days he lost count of everything. On his recovery he found that the Arabs were going to punish a native chief, Mirambo, who had been robbing caravans and burning villages on the road to Ujiji. Stanley made up his mind to go with them; and accordingly he left Kwihara with his caravan on July 29. At first the Arabs were successful; but soon afterwards Mirambo ambushed them in some thick giant grass, and defeated them with terrible slaughter. That night there was a scare in the camp that Mirambo was coming, and the whole Arab force fled in a panic. Stanley was awakened from sleep to find that all his men had joined the general rout except Selim, an Arab boy from Jerusalem. Stanley asked him why he had not also deserted his master. "Oh, sir," replied the lad, "I was afraid you would whip me."

Stanley at once gave chase, and tried to rally the Arab chiefs and make them stand their ground. Besides being a brave and fearless man, he was also a clever soldier, and he saw at a glance what ought to be done; but all was in vain, and he had to retreat with the rest to Unyanyembe. He collected his caravan, and fortified himself inside the mud walls of his house at Kwihara for more than a month. At last Stanley would wait no longer; so, leaving most of his stores at Kwihara, he started on September 20 with a light-laden caravan to move round the south of Mirambo's country and make a dash for Ujiji. Fever laid him on his back at the first camp; and twenty of his men, thinking him safely out of the way for a while, went back to Unyanyembe. In the morning Stanley was better, and he sent an escort to bring them back, but only half of them could be found. Stanley now got a long slave chain with nine collars from an Arab chief, and with this he threatened his men if any should desert again.

They started once more, but soon Shaw gave in, and was sent back with four men to Unyanyembe. Passing on in a country that looked like a rolling sea of green, yellow, and brown leafage, they came through Uganda and Manyara to the beautiful banks of the Igombe. The men were tired with their long marches, and Stanley halted for two days to rest and shoot game for food. After several hours of hunting, Stanley was very hot and dusty, and the cool waters of the Igombe tempted him to have a swim. He stripped himself, and was just about to dive into the deep water, when he saw the wicked eye and cruel jaw of a crocodile making ready for him in the bed of the river. Stanley was luckily just able to recover his balance, spring back, and escape.

When it was time to break up the camp, the men, who had been feasting on game like gluttons, were too lazy to move. They sent Bombay to ask Stanley for another day's halt; but the request was refused, as the next day they would have been lazier still. Bombay, who had been twice thrashed for playing truant at Unyanyembe, now turned sullen, and began to set the men against their master. Soon after starting, the men threw down their loads, and two of them came towards Stanley, with savage looks and with their rifles at the ready. It was a fateful moment for Stanley, but he was brave enough for anything. Levelling his rifle at the first mutineer, he ordered him to drop his weapon on the ground, and the man at once obeyed. The second, Asmani the Guide, was not so easily cowed, and he still came on with a look of murder in his eyes. For a moment Stanley thought he would have to take Asmani's life or lose his own, and possibly Livingstone's too. At this point Mabruki, who had been a faithful servant to Speke, struck down Asmani's rifle, and with a few words brought him to his senses. Then he called on the men to take up their loads and obey their master; for, though he might be a harsh one, did they not see how brave he was, and had he not filled them with meat? They promised to obey; and Stanley very wisely pardoned them all. His coolness and courage had won them over, and he had no more trouble with them.

After leaving the Igombe they made for the Malagazari River. The way led over valleys and ravines, with marsh in their hollows to such a depth that they were sometimes up to their shoulders in the muddy ooze. At one place the guide pointed out a quagmire, where a caravan of thirty-five men had disappeared for ever through the thin and shaking crust of grass and roots into the slush below.

They crossed the Malagazari in canoes, and, as usual, made the donkeys swim with a rope round their necks. While one of them was in the middle of the stream, the jaws of a large crocodile came suddenly above water and closed on the poor creature's throat. The men hauled hard on the rope, but to no purpose; the rope came away, but they saw the donkey no more.

At Uvinza they met a caravan which gave them the good news that Livingstone was not only alive, but had returned to Ujiji. These tidings were doubly joyous; for, if they were true, Livingstone would soon be relieved, and the difficult search through Central Africa would be avoided. Stanley now pressed forward with all speed; and in the beginning of November, eight months after leaving Bagamoyo, his caravan marched into Ujiji. The townsfolk crowded round them to hear their news, and to ask after friends at the war in Unyanyembe. Through the din of shouts and chatter in Arabic and native language, Stanley was startled to hear, "Good morning, sir," twice spoken in English. The words came from Susi and Chuma, two of Dr. Livingstone's most faithful men. They quickly led him to their master's hut, and soon Stanley was shaking hands with the greatest and noblest of all African explorers. Little did Stanley think at the time that he himself

THE JAWS OF A LARGE CROCODILE CLOSED ON THE POOR CREATURE'S THROAT.

was one day to finish the work of discovery this noble pioneer had begun.

Livingstone was in serious trouble. He had just tramped hundreds of miles to Ujiji, in hunger and in pain every step of the way, only to find his stores there plundered and sold. Fever, hardship, and toil had worn him to what he called "a mere tackle of bones," and his food was all but done. Stanley had arrived only just in time, and he never forget the joy of being able to restore Livingstone to health and comfort with the supplies he had brought through such dangers and difficulties. Stanley also brought from Unyanyembe a packet of letters, which, through the bad choice of bearers by the British Consul at Zanzibar, had already been more than a year on the road from the coast. The sight once more of his children's writing lit up the old man's haggard face with joy. "Ah!" he said, "I have waited years for letters, and have been taught patience."

Stanley was the first white man that Livingstone had seen for five years, so there was plenty of news to pass between them. After resting for some days they took a cruise in a canoe round the north end of Lake Tanganyika; for they wanted to see if there was a river running out of the lake towards the Nile. Every night they camped on shore, and they found this such an easy way of travelling that Livingstone called it their "picnic." They found that a river, the Rusizi, flowed into Tanganyika from a small lake, called Kivu, which lay in the hills to the northward. There was no time to go farther, for Stanley had to return;

so they came down the west shore to Cape Luvamba, and then crossed to Ujiji.

All this time Stanley had been learning many things from Livingstone's thirty years' experience of Africa; and once he had the chance of seeing the great man's wonderful power with the natives. At one of their camps on the shore of the lake the natives, who at first were friendly, afterwards tried to force on a quarrel. Their chief, who was a hopeless old scoundrel, wilfully cut his own leg with a spear and then swore that the strangers had done it. Even the rascal's own wife thought this trick so mean that she called him all the names she could think of, and advised him to make peace. A fight, however, seemed almost certain; but in the end Livingstone, with his gentle patience and fearless good humour, talked them over to friendship.

On their return to Ujiji, Stanley tried in vain to persuade his new friend to return to England. Livingstone had promised his friends in the Royal Geographical Society to try to find the sources of the Nile, and he was determined to keep his word. He might have already finished this work, if only honest bearers had been sent with his stores from Zanzibar instead of worthless slaves. However, he settled to go with Stanley as far as Unyanyembe, and wait there till his friend could send him a new set of bearers from Zanzibar.

Accordingly, on December 27, 1871, they left Ujiji; and, in order to avoid Mirambo's war, they went down the lake in canoes to Urimba, and then turned eastwards up the valley of the river Loageri. It was an unknown land even to their guide, who proved so useless that Stanley headed the caravan and steered by compass over hill and plain till they struck their former road. It was a rough journey and they suffered much from hunger, though they ate a buffalo, two zebras, and a giraffe by the way. Once Stanley had to take to his heels to escape from an elephant, and another time the whole caravan was stampeded for half a mile by a swarm of wild bees. Near the Igombe River they met a caravan which told them that Shaw had died of fever at Unyanyembe, and that Mirambo was besieged in his stockade by the Arabs.

At last, after fifty-three days, they reached Stanley's old quarters at Kwihara in Unyanyembe; and Livingstone once more found that his expected stores had been plundered by faithless bearers. Stanley, however, now gave him enough supplies to make forty loads, and he also promised to send up some good men to bear them. Then, after a short rest, Stanley started for the sea coast on March 14.

Their parting was a sad one, for they had grown to be great friends. Livingstone went a short distance with the caravan; but there was no use in delay, and they said good-bye. Stanley went on to the open world and his friends; but the brave old pioneer and saint turned back to his lonely death in the forest, having looked on the last white face he was ever to see.

Four months in the presence of this great man made quite a change in Stanley, and afterwards altered his life. In Livingstone he saw a man who was not only clever, fearless and strong, but also gentle, patient and just. He saw, too, how unselfishly the old explorer had gone through thirty years of toil and suffering, not for money or fame, but for love of doing good to men. Stanley could not help thinking of his new friend's heroic life; and the end of this was that, in a few years, he himself gave up his life to the noble and useful work of pioneering Africa for the good of mankind.

The journey to the sea was a hard one. At Mpwapwa, where Farquhar was found to have died, they came into the thick of the rainy season, which was worse than it had been for years. At the fords of the mountain streams they had to stretch a rope from bank to bank, and to this they clung while they stemmed the torrent with their packs on their heads. At Simbamwenni a hundred villages had been swept away in a single night; and for miles and miles the country was under swamp and flood. In the valley of the Makata, where they waded before, they now had to swim with their loads lashed to rafts. At one crossing a box holding all Livingstone's letters, diaries, and records for the last five years, was nearly swept down the river: that was a moment of suspense that Stanley never forgot. The jungle-tunnel, too, was knee-deep in mire, and all the snakes and scorpions in the land seemed to have collected within it. Now and then they saw a great boa hanging from a tree in wait for prey.

At last, on May 6, 1872, after thirteen months' travel, Stanley reached Zanzibar, and soon after returned to England. A few geographers and journalists in England and America said jealous and bitter things of Stanley; and the story was spread that he had never seen Livingstone at all. This unjust and unworthy treatment cut Stanley to the heart. But when Queen Victoria thanked him for his self-sacrifice and bravery, and when the Royal Geographical Society gave him their medal, he felt more able to forgive and forget what never should have been said.

A Pledge to Livingstone's Memory

Next year Stanley went to Coomassie as war correspondent with the British force sent to punish the King of Ashanti. On his way back to England in March 1874, he heard of the death of Livingstone, his hero and friend. The brave old pioneer had died at his post in the heart of Africa; and his faithful followers, who loved him for his kindness and care, went through nine months of danger and hardship while they bore his body to Zanzibar. Under the leadership of Susi and Chuma they had buried his heart at Chitambo's village on Lake Bangweolo. Then they had all sworn that his body should go back to the great Queen who had sent him to Africa, not to get gold and ivory and slaves, like the Arabs and Portuguese, but to give a good message of wisdom and to set men free. Livingstone's tomb in Westminster Abbey, where Stanley helped to carry him, shows how nobly these black men kept their word.

This event changed the course of Stanley's life. He looked upon Livingstone as the "Apostle of Africa" and the "daring pioneer" of its freedom; and now he pledged his life to carry on his old friend's work to the utmost of his power. Livingstone's heroic life and death turned all men's minds to African affairs; and in a short while Stanley was sent out by the *Daily Telegraph* and the *New York Herald*.

In September 1874 he was again at Zanzibar, this time preparing to finish what Speke, Burton and Grant had begun at the head-waters of the Nile, and then to carry on Livingstone's work on the Lualaba. Three white men came with him: Frank and Edward Pocock, the sons of a Kentish fisherman, and a young clerk named Barker. He also brought a light and roomy boat called the *Lady Alice*, which could be carried in eight pieces and easily put together. Most of his old followers joined him, and Manwa Sera, one of Speke's faithful men, was made chief. Others came too; and each man had to promise before his relations that he would be a true and obedient servant to his master. Stanley also had to promise "on the word of a white man" that he would treat them kindly and with patience, and that he would not abandon them when sick.

Stanley left Bagamoyo on November 17 with about three hundred and fifty men and a few of their wives. He now tried Livingstone's plan of treating the unruly ones with patience and forbearance, but still he had much trouble with his men. The first night at Bagamoyo he had to lock up twenty of them for running riot in the town; and it took him three hours to soothe the angry townsfolk, who came with drawn swords to ask for justice. Before reaching Mpwapwa fifty deserters had got away, and on the plains of Uhumba, fifty more planned to desert, but were stopped by the punishment of their ringleaders. Stanley was really well rid of the worthless deserters; and his milder treatment made the others repay him a thousand-fold in the time of his greatest need.

The caravan took the old route as far as Mukondoku in Ugogo, and then struck northwards for Lake Victoria Nyanza. The part of Ugogo they crossed was mostly unfertile and much of it wilderness. At first water was sometimes scarce till the rainy season came on; then famine set in, for by that time of year the crops were almost all eaten. At Itumbe they were digging for water in the sandy bed of a dry stream, when they saw a storm on the hills. No rain fell near them; but in half-an-hour a river, forty yards wide and eighteen inches deep, came rushing down, only to dwindle away to nothing in a few hours. Once, too, at dead of night Stanley woke from his sleep to see his boots sail gracefully out of his tent on a flood; while his two bull-terriers, "Bull" and "Jack," were fighting for the biggest share of sitting room on an island made of an ammunition box.

Food grew scarcer and scarcer; and when they entered the wide and deserted jungle of Uveriveri and headed for Suna, they indeed learnt what hunger meant. There was no track; and for several days they crushed their way through thickets of brushwood, thorn-scrub and stunted trees, thrusting aside the stubborn branches that tore their skin and clothing. The guide lost his way, and Stanley had to steer by compass. When the useless native again found his landmarks, they were at the village of Uveriveri, nearly worn out and starving, and Suna was still twenty-eight miles off.

Four men and a donkey laden with coffee had lagged behind the caravan and were lost in the bush; and Manwa Sera, with twenty men, was at once sent to find them. Three of the stragglers were found dead from hunger and fatigue, but the fourth man and the donkey could not be found. There was no food to be had in the village; and Stanley, who could scarcely bear to see the gaunt bones and hollow eyes of the faces that looked to him for help, asked for volunteers to bring supplies from Suna. He now found out what men, made faithful by kindness and justice, will do for a leader they trust and respect. Forty of his followers, worn and weak as they were, started at once to get food for their sick and exhausted companions.

Next day, after a dismal and hungry night, Stanley and those who were still able to move ranged the neighbour-hood in search of game, berries and roots, but without success. Some of the men, however, found the dead car-case of an elephant; and so cruel was their hunger, that they ate like wolves and were almost poisoned. Another night came, and still no food; but a happy thought made Stanley and Pocock look through the medical stores, and they found a quantity of fine meal for making gruel. Then there was joy on the famished faces of the men, who crowded round the camp fire, watching ten pounds of meal and twenty-five gallons of water, stirred round and round with a stick in a sheet-iron travelling-trunk. No watched pot ever seemed so long in boiling as this strange cauldron, but at last it seethed and bubbled, and then! It could not be called a meal; but for a while it stayed the dull and grinding pain at their waists, and gave them the strength to sleep.

Soon after nine o'clock that same night an eager ear heard a rifle shot in the far distance. It was the signal of the relief party; and in the early morning hours they came into camp, after tramping fifty-six miles in little more than a day and a half. They had only been able to bring enough millet to give the whole camp one meal. As soon as this was eaten, the plucky fellows insisted on starting at once, without further rest, so that the sick might reach Suna before nightfall.

From Suna they struggled on to Chiwyu where Edward Pocock died after a short illness. Famine still dogged their footsteps, and the caravan dragged its way into Vinyata like a file of spectres. Here they hoped to rest and recover, for food was more plentiful and the natives seemed friendly. Their Mganga, or "doctor of magic," brought an ox as a present, and was given four times its value in cloth and beads. Unluckily, some bales of wetted cloth had been spread out to dry; and Stanley saw his visitors give each other sly and suspicious looks.

Next day Stanley heard that two stragglers from the

IT COULD NOT BE CALLED A MEAL, BUT IT STAYED THE DULL PAIN AT THEIR WAISTS.

camp had been killed and a third badly wounded, and soon after a large body of armed natives gathered on a mound close at hand. Stanley at once told sixty men under Pocock to take axes and build a stockade round the camp, while he himself went out with some of the riflemen to parley with the natives. Stanley did all he could to avoid bloodshed; for, as he afterwards said, he remembered how Livingstone had taught him forbearance. At first he succeeded, but afterwards another body of natives came up and forced on a quarrel. They were a set of robbers and murderers, and were bent on plundering the caravan. With savage war cries they rushed to the attack, but after an hour's sharp fighting they were driven back.

By nightfall the stockade was finished and loopholed all round, with "marksman's nests" at each corner; and the cover was cut and cleared away for 200 yards, so that no one could creep up to the camp without being seen. Stanley had only seventy rifles, none too much ammunition, and no food; so the caravan could not stand a siege for long. Distant war cries, too, told that men were gathering against them from far and near.

At daybreak the natives attacked in force; and, after driving them off, Stanley determined to make a sally, in order to get supplies for his hungry camp. He divided his seventy riflemen into seven companies of ten, each under a chief. Four companies were stretched out in open order into a wide fighting line; two more were held behind in reserve, and one was left to guard the camp; and thus the plucky band under their dashing leader went out against hundreds of natives.

All seemed going on well, when unluckily the company on the right flank grew rash, lost order, and were killed to a man. This disaster at once brought the second and third companies into straits, and soon they became hard pressed and lost heavily. Ruin now seemed certain; but Stanley, who was a practised soldier, kept a cool head. He rushed forward fifteen reserves under the gallant Manwa Sera; thus they not only saved the day, but swept the country for some miles towards the native stronghold, sacking and burning several villages. Stanley's men had lost twenty-one killed and three wounded; but they brought plenty of goats, oxen, and grain to the camp, and famine was at an end for a while.

On the following day the natives again attacked in greater numbers than ever. After driving them off Stanley saw that he must force his way out of the country before he was overwhelmed by still larger numbers. Keeping his men well together, he followed the natives, stormed their stronghold, and scattered them to the hills, while he recaptured some of his lost rifles. Then, before they had time to recover, he returned to the caravan and pushed onward by quick marches to the friendly and fertile Usukuma land.

They had three days' rest at Mombiti, where Stanley rewarded his brave men to such an extent that they named him "the man with the open hand." Near the headwaters of the river Simiyu, the longest of the Nile sources, they came into a land of plenty; and in two days they shot one giraffe, one buffalo, two gnu, and six zebra. The natives were kind and helpful, though at one place their curiosity became a nuisance. One inquisitive chief rudely forced his way into the tent where the strange white man was having an afternoon nap. A chorus of yells and snarls woke Stanley to see that "Bull" and "Jack" had pinned the chief by the wrists, and were trying to tug his arms out of joint. Stanley released him, and he showed better manners for the future.

Moving on, they passed through a country of rich downs covered with short green grass, where thousands of cattle, sheep, and goats crowded the pastures. At Abaddi they were able to buy an ox for eighteen pennyworth of cloth, and a goat for sixpence, while fowls were a shilling a dozen!

At last the caravan came over a ridge and saw Speke's mighty lake, the Victoria Nyanza, glistening like silver from the shore beneath them to the sky-line. With loud shouts of joy and songs of thanksgiving, they hurried down the hillside and camped near the beach at Kageyi. It was now February 27, 1875, and they had come 720 miles in 103 days.

'BULL' AND 'JACK' PINNED THE CHIEF BY THE WRISTS.

The Victoria Nyanza

After a rest of nine days at Kageyi, Stanley set out in the *Lady Alice* to explore the coast of Victoria Nyanza. He chose a crew of eleven and made Safeni their chief, while the rest of his men were left in camp under the charge of Pocock, Barker, and Manwa Sera.

At his first halt he picked up a guide named Saramba, whose hair was like a huge mop, and whose whole outfit was a goat-skin round his loins and a spear in his hand. They went past the mouth of the Simiyu and along the eastern shore; and, after their long march from the sea-coast, they found it a pleasant manner of travelling. Still there were violent squalls of wind, rain, and hail, which tried them and their boat to the utmost; and the natives were often unfriendly, and sometimes very hostile. The herds of hippopotami that swarmed the lake were warlike and very ill-mannered, for they swam open-mouthed at their visitors, snapping their huge jaws together like pistol-shots. The voyagers kept well out of their way, for the woodwork of their boat was too light to withstand such powerful teeth. The islands of Kiregi seemed to be the nursery of all the crocodiles in the neighbourhood; and Stanley found one nest in the sand holding fifty-eight eggs. He also saw a large monitor, a kind of lizard, hunting for crocodile's eggs. On shooting it, Stanley found it measured seven feet from its beak-like nose to the tip of its tail.

The shores of the Nyanza were fertile and pleasing; and the frequent villages were surrounded with groves of date palms and bananas, while cattle and goats cropped the rich-coloured grass. But often the natives refused to sell food, and at Uvuma the party were attacked. Stanley had brought the *Lady Alice* close to the beach and was asking for a market, when a sudden volley of stones from the slings of the natives came whizzing about the ears of the crew. Some of the attacking party rushing into the water hurled chunks of rock, in the hope of smashing and sinking the boat, but these luckily fell short. Stanley then fired his revolver over their heads; and, while they fell back for a moment, the boat drew out of range. On passing the next point, however, a canoe shot out of a creek and lay across their bows, and its crew held up some sweet potatoes, which they most politely offered for sale.

While a bargain was being made, canoe after canoe came up, and soon the *Lady Alice* was surrounded. Stanley stood up and saw that there were only a few handfuls of potatoes in the first canoe, while the others were packed with spears. He now spoke to the natives with offers of friendship, but they answered with insult and scorn, and some of them grasped the blades of the oars, while others began to steal things out of the stern of the boat. He now warned them to let him go in peace, or they would find that the white man's gun could bite a long way off. It was all in vain, for they were murderous pirates, who would attend to nothing but force. A few shots fired overhead made them drop the oar blades, and Stanley's crew pulled ahead with all their might. Then a cloud of spears came flying through the air, but the men bent well down in the boat and no one was hit. The natives dashed after them, but a few bullets from Stanley's rifle made leaks in the foremost canoes, and they soon gave up the chase.

Soon after this adventure they explored the spot where Speke first saw the Victoria Nile leave the great Nyanza and plunge over the Ripon Falls on its way towards the sea. Beyond this river lay the land of Uganda, whose powerful king, Mtesa, at once sent the voyagers a hearty message of welcome. They landed at Usavara, and were met by one of the king's officers and a crowd of men in uniform, who at once escorted them to comfortable quarters. Then the officer said his master thought the white man might like a little food before their meeting; and presently fourteen fat oxen, sixteen sheep and goats, a hundred clumps of bananas, and other things on the same scale were brought. Stanley's crew of veterans soon made many friends; but the neat, uniformed servants of the king looked on poor mop-headed Saramba with scorn and contempt. Whence came such a slave, they asked, whom no one would buy for a ripe banana?

King Mtesa soon took a great liking to Stanley, or

"Stamlee" as he pronounced the name; and he questioned the explorer by the hour about the ways and ideas of white men. One day he invited Stanley to a naval review, at which all his officers and about 200 ladies of his court were present. A squadron of forty beautifully made canoes were each manned by thirty men, and they went through their drill in wonderful style. Then Mtesa heard that a young crocodile was asleep in the sun by the shore of the lake. "Now, Stamlee," he said, "show my women how white men can shoot." Stanley took his elephant gun, which carried a heavy three-ounce bullet, and delighted his host by killing the crocodile outright with his first shot.

On the invitation of the kind Mtesa, Stanley now set out to bring the rest of his expedition to Usavara; and one of the king's admirals, Magassa, was ordered to take thirty canoes and go with him. Magassa, however, let Stanley go on in advance and promised to overtake him, but he failed to keep his word, and nearly brought them to ruin. This time they went by the western shore of the Nyanza; but when they were a few days beyond the Uganda country, the natives again became unfriendly. Time after time food was refused them; and when at last they reached an island, named Bumbire, they had been fasting nearly two days.

The voyagers made for a stretch of shingle which lay between the water's edge and a steep grassy bank, beyond which their hungry eyes could see banana groves and huts. But here again they were greeted with war cries by the natives, who crowded on the bank, waving their spears and twanging their bow-strings. Stanley would now have retired; but the famished Safeni pleaded so piteously for a "shauri" or parley, that the order was given to row gently towards the shore. Safeni stood up and spoke like an orator. Soon the spears were lowered, the war cries died away, and fifty natives came down the beach with smiling faces and offers of friendship and food.

As the boat grounded they crowded round her in the water, and began to ask friendly questions and to talk of the price of bananas. Next moment a swarm of black hands gripped the gunwale of the boat and hauled her high and dry twenty yards up the beach before her crew knew they were caught. Then with savage yells and shrieks of hideous laughter these fiends began their war dance round the prisoners, twanging their bow-strings, flourishing their spears, and whirling aloft their knob-sticks and clubs.

Stanley saw that it was useless to resist, for all would be killed before they could load their rifles. They could do nothing but wait in patience, and, if need be, die bravely. Presently the natives closed in, and one of the boat's crew was struck on the back with a knob-stick, while other strokes were ready to fall. Stanley was on the point of using his revolver, when their chief, Shekka, appeared and drove them all back with his stick. Then, taking the elders of his tribe apart from the rest, he sat down on the bank to have a "shauri."

Stanley could not speak their language, so he sent Safeni with some of the best cloth and beads, telling him to say there was more in the white-man's camp, if Shekka became his friend. The "shauri" lasted a long while, and Safeni did the utmost his eloquence could do; but he returned to the boat with a gloomy face, saying he thought they were bad men, for they would promise nothing. In a few moments a number of natives again surrounded them and suddenly snatched away the oars. Then Shekka told Safeni they were going away for a while to have a feast of good things and to talk the matter over, after that they would return and say what they meant to do. Thus they disappeared over the bank, but not before setting a watch over their starving prisoners.

About the middle of the afternoon the natives again gathered on the bank in greater numbers than before. Their heads were bristling with war feathers, and it was now plain what they were going to do. There was one chance left, and Stanley saw he must try it at once. Sending Safeni towards the bank with a piece of the gaudiest cloth, he bade his men surround the boat, while he himself sat inside and watched the enemy. As soon as the bright colour caught the greedy eyes of the natives, he quietly gave the word to his men, who at once bent their backs and tugged with might and main to launch the *Lady Alice*. Would she never move? The stress of the moment seemed to double their strength, and Stanley now began to hear the joyful music of her keel upon the grinding shingle. The natives heard it too, and, with howls of fury, dashed down the bank towards the beach; while the gallant Safeni ran for his life on a warning shout from his master, who was now slipping cartridges into the elephant gun. Faster and faster the boat sped down the shingle, on through the shallow, and out into the deep, with her crew clinging to her gunwale in the water; and for the moment they were safe.

But poor Safeni, running like an ostrich, was only at the water's edge, and two spearmen were close at his heels. Calling out to him to throw himself down into the water, Stanley fired over his head. The bullet killed the first man and, passing on, disabled the second. This checked the rush of the spearmen; but arrows began to whizz from the bank, till two charges of duck-shot made the bowmen shift their ground. During this lull Stanley hauled one man into the boat, and with this extra help the whole crew were soon safely on board. The men were getting out the rifles when their master told them to tear up the boards that lined the bottom of the boat and to use them for paddles as best they could, for more trouble was close at hand.

Two canoes were already launched, two more were quickly following; and a pair of angry hippopotami, wakened from sleep by the riot, were coming open-mouthed for the boat. Stanley waited till the animals were only ten yards away before he fired, for he dared not risk a miss. Right and left the poor brutes sank like stones, and he was free to meet his human enemies. Once more the elephant gun did as his quick eye and steady nerve directed, and the heavy bullets ripped and splintered the thin sides of the canoes. After four shots the two foremost canoes filled and sank; and the others, after picking up their friends, dared come no farther.

The natives now crowded to a point round which the *Lady Alice* had to pass; but when their arrows fell short of the boat they shrieked with rage. "Go," they screeched with angry curses, "go and die in the Nyanza!"

The boat's crew had now been without food for more than two days. There was a dead calm, and their rough paddles only made three-quarters of a mile an hour. Soon a fair breeze sprang up, and they were able to sail eight miles before it dropped. By chopping up a thwart they managed to boil some coffee, and then they lay down to bear all night the pains of hunger as best they could. Next morning no land was in sight; but in the evening, after being three whole days without food, they reached an uninhabited island. They named it Refuge Island; and Stanley with five of the men at once went to look for supplies. Stanley soon returned with a brace of wild duck; two of the men brought a load of delicious berries, while another pair came back with two great clumps of bananas. These things with some coffee made them once more feel like men.

Next day they rested while a tree was cut down to make oars, and then their voyage was continued. At last, on May 6, they reached the camp at Kageyi, but their hearty welcome was spoilt by the news that Barker and Speke's faithful Mabruki had died. In fifty-seven days the *Lady Alice* had voyaged right round the great Nyanza, a distance of 1000 miles.

FROM UGANDA TO NYANGWÉ

Stanley now prepared to move his camp into Uganda, as Mtesa had advised; but the faithless Magassa never came with the necessary canoes. Meanwhile, Stanley was struck down with a bad attack of fever, which left him weak and thin. As soon as he was able to get up, he went to a neighbouring chief, Lukongeh, in the hope of buying or hiring canoes for the voyage. The chief was very friendly and civil, but he was never in a hurry about anything, except to go for his meals. So Stanley was told to "go and get fat," while Lukongeh thought the matter over.

This did not look very hopeful; but, after a long wait, the chief lent his new friend "Stamlee" enough canoes to carry half his camp, though they proved to be the worst and oldest of all his fleet. The canoes of the Nyanza were made of thin boards, laced together with cane fibre, and the seams were caulked with a kind of putty made of pounded banana stalk. Stanley told some of his followers to patch up Lukongeh's canoes; and then, on June 20, he started for Refuge Island, with 150 men and half his stores.

Their first night's camp was to be on an islet, and they had to push on after dusk to reach it. Suddenly Stanley heard the desperate cry, "Bring the boat, master; we're sinking!" Hurrying to the spot, he found that a canoe had sunk, and her crew were struggling in the water. The rotten cane fibre had given way, and a heavy box of ammunition had fallen through the bottom, and she had filled in a moment.

Scarcely had Stanley picked up the men, when the same cry was heard a few hundred yards away, "The boat, master! the boat!" The lacing of a second canoe had ripped open, and her crew could not bale her out fast enough to keep her afloat. These also were taken aboard the Lady Alice, who was now loaded down to her gunwale, when another, and yet another cry for help came ringing over the water. Telling the canoe-men to bale for their lives, Stanley hurried the boat towards the island. It seemed as if they would never be there; but at last she grounded, and after being speedily emptied, she was raced back to the rescue.

It was pitch dark when they returned to the sinking canoes; and to see what was going on, Stanley had to light, one by one, the leaves of a book he had brought to read on the way. Thus fumbling their way from sound to sound, they managed to save all the lives; but they lost five canoes, five rifles, some ammunition, and 1200 lbs. of grain.

On reaching Refuge Island, Stanley sent back for the rest of his camp; and in this same manner he moved all his men and stores to Mahyiga, an isle close to Bumbiré. Here they were joined by a large search party, sent in canoes by the anxious Mtesa. Magassa had gone as far as Bumbiré, where the natives told him the story that the *Lady Alice* had been lost in the Nyanza during a storm. They also gave up the oars, and said these were all that remained of the boat and her unlucky crew! The lazy Magassa was only too glad to believe them, and returned home to his bananas and palm wine. Mtesa, however, knew the Bumbiré pirates too well to listen to such a tale, and he at once sent out a strong party to look for his friend "Stamlee."

Meantime, the Bumbiré natives had collected in force, with many friends from the mainland; and, when the men of Uganda sent a message of peace, they murdered the messenger. Then they sent an impudent message back, to say they were coming to kill all the strangers and eat up their goods.

Stanley dared not risk an attack on the water, for the natives might upset some of his heavy-laden canoes and sink his precious stores. Taking, therefore, only his armed men and Mtesa's warriors, he sailed to Bumbiré, and in a one-sided fight punished the pirates severely. Next day he was allowed to go on his way in peace; and on August 12 pitched a new camp at Dumo, in Uganda.

The message now came that Mtesa was at war with Uvuma, whose people had attacked Stanley a few months before. No one was ever allowed to leave the country when the king was at war, so Stanley left his caravan at Dumo, and went to look on at the fighting. On the way to

Mtesa's army, at the Ripon Falls, poor "Jack," one of the bulldogs, was killed by a fierce native cow which had run wild. "Jack" tried to pin her; but, missing his grip, was crushed against a tree-trunk by her long, sharp horns. "Bull" and "Jack" were great friends, though sometimes they had quarrelled, but never seriously, about the first choice of bones or the best place to sleep. "Bull" now walked several times round the body of his companion, sniffing it well to make sure that he was dead; then he sat down on his haunches beside his friend, with his great, moist eyes staring blankly into space, as though trying to think out the great puzzles of his life.

Mtesa's army of 150,000 men and 325 canoes held a camp on the shore, looking over a narrow strait to an island on which the enemy had gathered. The Waganda, a word which means "people of Uganda," fought best on land; while the Wavuma, or "people of Uvuma," were much better sailors. Mtesa and Stanley sat on a hillside overlooking the straits, and watched great canoe fights every few days.

Between whiles the two men talked about many things, and especially of the religion of Christ; for Mtesa promised Stanley to become a Christian and have a mission station in his land.

One day an important chief of the Wavuma was taken prisoner, and Mtesa ordered him to be tied to a stake and burnt. Stanley, however, told the King that this was not loving his neighbour as himself; and Mtesa, after much persuasion, let the man go. Stanley was always being asked many questions of very different kinds. Once he was called upon to tell all the Waganda chiefs what an angel was like. Another time he was asked: "Stamlee, how is that the white men have long noses, while their dogs have very short noses; while almost all black men have short noses, but their dogs have very long noses?"

After many battles had been fought, Stanley helped Mtesa to make peace with the Wavuma, and he was then allowed to depart. Mtesa, who was very sorry to lose his friend, gave him many presents, amongst which were six walking-sticks and four white monkey skins. Stanley wanted to explore a lake called Muta Nzigé, now known as the Albert Edward Nyanza, and Mtesa sent one of his generals, Sambuzi, to escort him thither.

Stanley now broke up his camp at Dumo, and marched up the river Katonga till he met Sambuzi. Then on January 1, 1876, they crossed the border of Uganda; and, marching through the grand hill country of Ankolé, they at last came in sight of the Muta Nzigé. They encamped on a plateau overlooking the lake, with fifty feet of cliff between them and its shore, and there was no way down which the boat could be carried to the water. The natives were unfriendly, and at once sent a message to say they were coming to fight. Sambuzi and his men turned cowards and insisted on a retreat, and Stanley was obliged to go with them. On reaching the Katonga, Stanley left Sambuzi and set out for Ujiji, intending to explore the rest of Lake Tanganyika and Livingstone's river, the Lualaba.

There were no very great adventures on the way to Ujiji. Stanley spent a month in the Karagwé country, exploring the Kagera or Alexandra Nile, which is the largest, though not the longest, of the Nile sources. The people of Karagwé lived mainly on milk, and were strong, healthy, and gentle; for the tribes who eat the most meat are generally the most cruel and vicious. Their king, Rumanika, sent Stanley to the hot springs of Mtagata, where all the black invalids of the neighbouring countries went for the good of their health. There were six springs of different heat; and Stanley had the choice of many hot pools: while among the over-hanging trees baboons and long-tailed monkeys grinned, and gibbered, and chattered about the funny white creature who could take off his skin and put it on again after his bath.

On April 7, Stanley came to the top of a ridge overlooking the wide valley of the river Malagarazi. The rain-drops which fell behind him trickled towards the Nile on their way to the Mediterranean Sea; while those falling in front of him drained southward to Tanganyika.

While moving on through Usambiro, Stanley lost another of his best friends; for here his other bulldog did its last day's march, after tramping 1500 miles of African soil. The faithful "Bull" had a fine character. He never worried or fussed about anything; but he did everything in earnest. He seldom spoke; but, whenever he did, the men gripped their rifles, for they knew "Bull" never called "danger" for nothing. When there was trouble he was always on the spot, grimly and quietly doing his best; and he never seemed either very pleased or very disappointed with what he had done. In the fight at Vinyata he had been in the forefront of the battle, and no native dared face him. He grew worn out with the heat and toil of the journey, but he never showed it to any one, and the day he died he was trotting doggedly on in his usual place. Quite unexpectedly he sank on the ground and gave a look upward, as though to beg pardon for thus breaking down. Then, as if he meant his spirit ever to be in the vanguard, he fixed his big, wistful eyes down the forward track till the light faded from them in death.

While Stanley was resting at Serombo, the great warrior Mirambo, who now had made peace with the Arabs, came to pay a friendly visit to his brother, the chief of the town. The night before his arrival the big drums were beaten to make silence among the three thousand townsfolk in the streets. Then, with the jangling of iron bells, the pompous town-crier shouted the following: "Listen, O men of Serombo! Mirambo, the brother of Ndega, cometh in the morning! Be ye prepared therefore, for his young men are hungry! Send your women to dig potatoes, dig potatoes! Mirambo cometh! Dig potatoes, potatoes, potatoes, dig potatoes, to-morrow!"

Stanley made friends with Mirambo, and this saved him from a great deal of trouble with the natives on the way to Ujiji, where he arrived without mishap on May 27. Here he launched his boat, and made a voyage round the south end of Tanganyika, for he had already explored the northern end with Livingstone in 1871. He carefully examined the Lukuga creek, where Cameron in 1874 thought he saw an out-flowing river choked up with giant reeds. Stanley found out that there was no real river, but only a river-bed, down which the waters of Lake Tanganyika could run whenever they rose high enough to overflow.

Returning to Ujiji, Stanley now prepared to explore the Lualaba downwards from Nyangwé, the farthest point that Livingstone had reached. More than forty of his men now deserted him; but with the remainder, about 150 in number, he arrived at Nyangwé in safety on October 27. Near this place he met a famous Arab trader, Tippu Tib, who for £1000 promised to escort Stanley for sixty days' march with 400 followers. And thus Stanley made ready for the hardest journey he had yet known.

Livingstone's River

On November 5th, 1876, Stanley left Nyangwé to follow Livingstone's great river towards the sea. Livingstone had taken measurements of its height above the sea-level; and, if his levels were correct, it could not reach the Nile without flowing uphill. Stanley's object was to see whether this mighty stream, which Livingstone's native guides had called a long lake full of islands, would turn out to be the Congo.

With Tippu Tib and his men as an escort, Stanley and his caravan plunged into the thick forest of Mitamba, which lay before them for many miles. Behind them they left the brilliant tropical sunshine, and for days and days they marched in twilight. The tops of the forest timber were so matted with leaves and creepers that the sun was shut out; while a pioneer party with axes had to cut a path through the thick undergrowth for the load-bearers. Every morning from dawn till ten o'clock the dew dripped off the trees like heavy rain and soaked everything through, while the soil became slippery with muddy clay. There were many wild beasts, monkeys and snakes; and one day they killed a python twice as long as an average man.

They passed through several villages, but the natives

seemed more like wild animals than men. In one of their main streets Stanley counted 186 skulls set on the ground in a double row, grinning at each other across a pathway ten feet wide. At first he thought he was in cannibal country, but that was a horror to come a few days later. The bones proved to be those of the gorilla, called "soko" by the natives, who are fond of its flesh.

In a fortnight they reached the river again at a point only forty-one miles from Nyangwé, and all were nearly worn out with the toil of forcing their way through the forest. Not quite three miles a day was a hopeless rate of travel; so Stanley now put some of his men into the boat, and went forward by river. The rest of the party with less to carry could now move faster along the bank.

Villages were very frequent; but at first the people fled into the woods howling their war-cry, "Ooh-hu-hu-hu-hu!" Here and there among the deserted huts the explorers saw horrible sights that told them they were now in cannibal country. Farther down the river the natives were fiercer and bolder, and seldom a day passed without an attack on the boat; for in their cruel ignorance the men of this godless land looked on the stranger as prey for a feast.

Smallpox and other sickness broke out, and soon there were seventy-two cases on the list. All that Stanley could do was to take them into the canoes and doctor them as best he could. At Ikondu they were lucky enough to find an old deserted canoe, which had been made out of a single tree of enormous size; when mended and fitted up as a "hospital ship" it held no less than sixty people.

The farther they went, the worse things became. No food could be bought; and almost every day they had to run the gauntlet through poisoned arrows and spears, while the big war-drums were seldom silent for long. At last Tippu Tib and the land party were delayed in the woods and dropped two days' march behind. The natives of Vinya Njara took the chance and attacked the boat in force with a fleet of canoes.

While the rifles were driving back the canoes, Stanley landed a party with axes, who soon made a rough camp, with a stockade and shelters of brushwood. Here all took refuge, and then for two hours they withstood a furious attack from the land side. Long after their repulse the natives kept on shooting poisoned reed arrows from the cover of the forest; but if any one was struck, Stanley at once burnt the wound with caustic and the poison did little harm.

At night each half of the band kept watch in turn, while two men with buckets of water were told to douse the heads of the worn-out watchers, whose eyes were heavy with sleep. At dead of night a native was seen creeping on his stomach like a lizard towards the camp. The brave Uledi, coxswain of the *Lady Alice*, at once wriggled out through the stockade and crept stealthily behind the enemy like a cat stalking a bird. Nearer and nearer the native crawled, thinking how well he was doing it, when

Uledi suddenly pounced on his back, pinned him by the arms and hustled him into camp. The howls of the prisoner brought on another furious attack from the forest; and, while the natives were being driven back, one of the riflemen was killed by a spear.

Stanley learnt from the captive that there was a village just a few hundred yards downstream; and at dawn he and his little band went quickly down the river and took it by storm. They soon fortified the village and carried the sick into huts; and then they defended themselves till midday, when with a desperate sally they drove the natives far into the woods. Three hours were now spent in cutting the cover all round the village; then at last the weary and famished men took half-an-hour for rest and food before they began to make marksman's nests all round the village. All night long poisoned arrows whizzed into the village, while the thumping of big war-drums roused the country on both sides of the river.

Next morning the fight began again, both from the forest and from a large fleet of canoes in the river; but, thanks to their defence works, Stanley's men easily held their own. Later on in the day Tippu Tib came up, and the natives retreated in their canoes behind an island across the river. Late that night, when the enemy seemed to be sleeping, Stanley sent Pocock with four canoes across the river to wait in the channel below the island. He himself crossed higher upstream with the *Lady Alice* and her crew; then, floating silently down in the shadow of the wooded bank, they cut adrift all the canoes they could find. As fast as they drifted down Pocock and his men picked them up, till in the end thirty-six fine canoes were towed back to camp in triumph. Next morning the natives made peace and brought food for Stanley's men, and then their canoes were returned.

The voyagers now rested a week at Vinya Njara; and Christmas was spent in canoe racing, while Tippu Tib gave a modest feast to all the men. Tippu Tib now broke his agreement, and refused to go any farther than this point; and on December 28th Stanley started again down the river with his party reduced to 149, of whom only forty had guns.

Fighting began again the very next day, and a new war-cry told the explorers that they were among a different people. They had passed through the country whose war-cry was "Ooh-hu-hu-hu-u-u!" and now they were in the land of "Bo-bo-bo-bo-o-o!" The cannibal natives attacked boldly in canoes, shouting savagely, "Meat! meat! Aha! Now we shall have plenty of meat! Bo-bo-bo-bo-o-o!" No sooner had the strangers driven off one set than the fight was taken up by the villages downstream. In vain did Stanley hold up necklaces and coils of wire while shouting "Sen-nen-eh! sen-nen-eh!"—the native word for peace. "Shall we give up so much meat for a few shells and some copper?" was the scornful reply.

Opposite one village a large canoe, 85 feet long, whose crew were painted half white and half red with broad black bars across, came dashing towards the *Lady Alice*. Stanley's men fired a volley at short range and then rushed the boat at the canoe. The natives escaped into the water, but Stanley caught the canoe and added it to his fleet.

On January 4th they heard in front of them the roar of rushing waters, and came to a series of seven cataracts with rapids between them, and they named them the "Stanley Falls." Where it was possible, the boat and canoes were run down the foaming current with a few men inside to steer them, while they were steadied with ropes of twisted rattan cane held by the men on the bank. When the dashing torrent was too dangerous, a path was cleared through the jungle with axes, and the canoes were dragged over land.

It took more than three weeks to pass the Stanley Falls; for at almost every cataract they had to fight for a footing on the bank before they could begin their work. The ropes frequently broke, and once a canoe got adrift. Zaidi, the man who was steering it, was all but swept over a cataract, but just managed to cling to a rock on the lip of the fall. Brave Uledi and Marzouk were let down the stream in a tethered canoe; but the moment Zaidi caught the rope thrown by one of the gallant pair the canoe broke adrift. Luckily she dashed against a rocky islet between Zaidi and the shore. Uledi and Marzouk sprang out and hauled Zaidi after them; and here they remained all night with a swirling rapid around them through which no man could possibly swim. Next morning, after many failures, the

A LARGE CANOE DASHING TOWARDS THE *LADY ALICE*.

men on shore managed to get a rope over to the island, where Uledi quickly made it fast to a rock. Then one by one the three castaways pulled themselves hand over hand through the racing waters, and reached the bank, half drowned but safe.

After clearing the Stanley Falls they had a fight every day for five days, and came to a people who had a new war-cry but still called for "meat." The voyagers had left behind them the land of "Ooh-hu-hu-hu" and "Bo-bo-bo-bo," and were now come to the realms of "Yaha-ha-ha-a-a." To their great surprise they came, on February 8th, to a place called Rubunga, where the people were quite friendly and gave them bananas and fish. Stanley asked their chief what the river was called at this part of its course, and the answer was "Congo."

At length, after more than thirty fights, they fought their last battle; and as their enemies used muskets, they knew that the country was now reached by trade from the west coast. Three days later the river ran into a wide basin surrounded by white chalk cliffs and full of islands. This they named Stanley Pool; and, passing on, they soon knew by the sight of mountains and the sound of rushing water, that more cataracts were ahead. The hardest of their toil was yet to come, for these were the rapids now known as the Livingstone Falls.

Down the Rapids to the Sea

The river now ran down a gorge with hills on either side for more than 150 miles. Often the gorge widened into a valley, whose steep slopes were covered with grass, fern, brushwood, and timber; and here were long smooth reaches, broken now and then by swift but passable rapids. But sometimes the hills closed in and cramped the broad stream into a narrow cataract. Here the raging waters chafed and fumed between sheer crags, or fought with deafening fury against the jutting bedrock and the giant boulders that lay piled in hundreds beneath the cliffs.

There were also many falls. Some dropped from terrace to terrace, or plunged into a seething pool. Others shot sloping downward into a mighty basin, where ridge after ridge of white-plumed waves lay across the breast of the current, on either side of which were great whirlpools ready to suck down all that drifted into their swirling hollows.

The explorers spent four weary months in passing this part of the river; and had the natives been hostile, they never could have succeeded. They were able to shoot many of the rapids in their canoes, though very skilful handling was needed to clear the rocks and eddies and to make a safe landing when the river became dangerous. It was risky work, and many canoes were lost, sometimes through accident, sometimes because the men grew too confident and became rash. Once, against Stanley's orders, a canoe went down the middle of a furious stream; and two others, thinking by this example that all was safe, followed in her wake. All three canoes and nine men were swept over a fall and never seen again.

At some of the more difficult places the canoes were steadied from the shore by ropes of twisted cane. This was very anxious toil, for the rocks and boulders gave slippery foothold and the rope often broke. Stanley and six men were one day in the *Lady Alice*, taking her in this way down a rapid, which afterwards became a cataract and shot over a low fall into a large pool. Suddenly the stern rope broke, and the boat swung broadside to the current. This sudden strain tore the middle ropes from the hands on shore and jerked a man out of the boat. While Stanley was hauling him on board the bow rope parted, and the *Lady Alice* was adrift on the racing stream.

It was well for the boat and her crew that Uledi was in her, for truly he was the hero of that fatal river. Not only had he saved many a canoe-load by his skill as a steersman, but more than a dozen times he had plunged in to bring drowning men safe ashore. Stanley had barely time to shout for him to take the tiller before the boat was darting down the cataract, where, in the din and strife of clashing waters, no human voice could possibly be heard. Their only hope, and that a feeble one, was to keep her end-ways in the smoother flood and clear the wild hazards in their course as best they could. The dark cliffs, rising 300 feet to the sky-line, seemed to spring out of the distance and slip behind them; while the massive boulders, piled along the edges of the cataract, were gliding past like a march of phantoms.

Here the boat narrowly missed a rocky islet wreathed in breakers and veiled in spray; there she just escaped the angry pucker and double tail of surf that fringed the eddy below a sunken reef. Then all in a moment she ran up the side of a rounded hump of water; but, ere she was well down the opposite slope, the hump settled into a hollow and the water began to wheel round—they were over a whirlpool.

Bending the oars with desperate strength, they managed to hold their own, though for a while the stern hung over a deep pit of swirling waters with a dark vortex-hole in the middle. In a few seconds the giant throat of the whirlpool began to refill with a horrible choking gurgle, till the hump once more replaced the hollow, and then the boat flew forward on her course.

At the neck of the cataract nearing the fall she went out of control and slewed round and round several times. Then, coming again under Uledi's guidance, she darted like an arrow down the centre of the slope, over wave after wave into the basin on an even keel. Here Uledi shot her off the tail of the downward flood into the return current of a vast eddy, which swept her near a strip of sand, where with a few good strokes she was grounded in safety.

Her crew jumped ashore and looked at each other, wondering how and why they happened to be alive. In about fifteen minutes they had come more than three miles, and Uledi's aching muscles knew best who had done most to save them. It took four days to bring the other vessels to the same spot. The holes between the boulders were filled with brushwood, and over this the canoes were dragged along beneath the cliff.

In this way they worked down the river bit by bit, but at the Inkissi Falls they found that the cliffs rose straight out of the water, with hills above them to the height of 1200 feet. There was no way by the river, so Stanley said he would go over the mountain. On hearing this the natives spread the report that he could make his canoes fly, and they shut up their pigs, goats, and fowls, lest the "white man's magic" should harm them. Two or three of the lighter canoes were soon drawn up the hill without any evil "magic" befalling their animals. Then about six hundred natives joined in the work, and soon all the canoes were again in the river below the Inkissi Falls. These natives had British crockery and other wares in their huts, and from this point onwards they were not at all eager to take Stanley's cloth and beads in payment for food. In this way food again became scarce, and hunger was added to the hardships of the rapids. Besides all this, nine canoes had already been lost, and Stanley was forced to halt while he made some more. Thus in two months he had scarcely passed through eighty miles of the gorge.

The next great trouble came where a long and wild rapid rushed over the Massassa Falls into a stormy basin. Stanley had gone forward with the baggage to choose a camp and make friends with the natives. Before starting he told Uledi to take nine men in a big canoe, called the Jason, and to pioneer the rapid as far as he thought safe. Just as the canoe was pushing off, Pocock decided to go in her, though he really ought to have stayed with the rest of the fleet. Uledi took the Jason halfway down the rapid and then put into a creek, beyond which both he and Manwa Sera said it was madness to venture. Pocock, however, thought he saw a safe way, and he hastily called Uledi a coward. "See," answered Uledi indignantly, holding up his hands, "all my fingers will not count the number of lives I have saved on this river." But Pocock had his own way, and Uledi at length asked his crew if they were ready to die in the river. "Our fate is in the hands of God," they answered, taking their places in the canoe. "Bismillah, in the name of God," said Uledi as the Jason shot out of the creek.

In a few moments poor Pocock saw that they must be swept over the fall; and, in bitter regret, he felt he could never forgive himself for his headstrong mistake. But there was no going back, and Uledi once more set himself to do all that remained to be done. If he could shoot the canoe end-ways into the basin, there was still just

POPCOCK WAS DRAWN DOWN.

a chance of life. With his wonderful skill he steered her past all dangers and headed her straight for the middle of the fall. True as an arrow she shot into the pool and darted forward; but a wave leapt up and tossed her aside into a whirlpool as though she were a twig. Then, after coursing a few times round and round the deepening hollow, she tilted on end and was sucked down into the whirling vortex.

In a few seconds the whirlpool refilled, and the Jason shot keel uppermost to the surface. The men swarmed from beneath her like otters and scrambled astride of her keel; but Uledi could only count eight of her crew, and Pocock was gone. While they were struggling to right the canoe, a second whirlpool refilled and threw up the missing white man. In a moment Uledi sprang from the canoe and dashed through the water to aid him; but, before he could reach the spot, the whirlpool began again. Uledi might well have turned back; yet still the noble fellow swam on, and plunged over the edge and into the dreadful hollow to do his best and die if need be. It was all in vain, for Pocock was drawn down the vortex and Uledi followed him.

When next the whirlpool refilled, Uledi rose to the surface and regained the canoe, but they never saw Pocock again. The Jason could not be righted, so they left her and swam ashore. Many days afterwards she was found farther down the river broken in half.

This adventure brought gloom over the camp and broke

the spirit of many men. Soon afterwards thirty-one of them refused to go farther and deserted in a body. Stanley let them go, and in a few days they were thankful to return. Then the party again struggled onwards; but food grew scarcer and scarcer, for the natives would not sell. When at last, towards the end of July, they reached the Isangila Falls they were all like gaunt and bony spectres. Stanley found out that this fall was the one Captain Tucky had reached from the sea in 1816, and it was needless to explore the river any farther. So the poor *Lady Alice*, which had travelled nearly 7000 miles, was carried to the top of the cliff and left to her fate; and on August 1, 1877, the caravan started on foot for Boma, near the mouth of the Congo.

The hunger they suffered on this march was terrible. The natives would scarcely look at Stanley's cloth and beads in payment for food, and the travellers soon found out what they wanted instead. They had just passed through a village when a chief and fifty armed men ran after them. Stanley turned to meet them; whereupon the chief sat down on a three-legged stool in the pathway, and pompously said—

"Know you I am king of this country?"

Stanley asked what tribute he might require.

"Rum," answered the king; "I want a bottle of rum."

Stanley looked so surprised that Uledi asked him what the king had demanded.

"He wants rum, Uledi; just think of it!" replied Stanley.

"Rum!" said Uledi wrathfully; "there's rum for him!"

Saying this he slapped his majesty's face with such force that he fell off his three-legged throne into the dust. His fifty subjects fled in dismay with their king at their heels, and nothing more was heard about tribute.

For more than a week the travellers went starving in a district where a bottle of rum would have bought more food than they could eat. "We don't want wire," the natives said; "if you have got rum you can have plenty of food." The natives were too ignorant and too weak-minded to use even their own palm-wine temperately, and drinking spirits often drove them into disease and ruin, if not to crime. Indeed, to give a native a bottle of ruin was like putting sweet poison into the hands of a child. Yet there were many white men whose greed for money led them into this selfish way of trade.

In a few days the caravan broke down from want of food, and Stanley sent Uledi forward to Boma with a letter asking for speedy help. Uledi was not long in returning with a party of bearers loaded with good things; and then the starving band had the first hearty meal they had tasted for more than a month. At last, on August 6, 1877, they reached Boma, on the 999th day from Zanzibar.

Stanley did not stay long in Boma, but started almost immediately to take his men by sea round the Cape to their homes. At the end of November they reached Zanzibar, and Stanley then returned to England. It was not long, however, before he was back on African soil.

'RUM!' SAID ULEDI; 'THERE'S RUM FOR HIM!'

Back to the Congo

By tracing Livingstone's river down to the sea, Stanley had found a possible way into the heart of the fertile country which that brave old pioneer had found. Other men now prepared to follow and make use of this rich land, and among the foremost of these was Leopold of Belgium. With the help of men from several different nations, he formed a society to open Central Africa to the trade of the world, and to put down slavery and cannibalism. The society was called the International Association of the Congo, and Stanley was sent in charge of an expedition to begin its work.

Early in 1879 Stanley started for Zanzibar, where he gathered his old followers and others, and in August of the same year he once more reached Boma. This time, however, he was not worn out and starving, but he had everything a pioneering party could possibly need, as well as three small river steamers which could be carried overland in pieces. He went up the river as far as he could, and landed his things at the foot of the Livingstone Falls. Here he made a station at Vivi on the hillside above the stream, and then the real work of the expedition began.

For about fifty miles above Vivi the river was impassable by boat as far as the top of the Isangila Fall, where Stanley had left the *Lady Alice* in 1877. The first thing to be done was to make a good road past this lower stretch of falls to the easier waters above them. The black labourers set to work under the direction of Stanley and eleven white men from different nations, and after many months of hard cutting, levelling, blasting, stone-breaking, bridging, and draining, at last the road was finished. In a little less than a year the steamers were floating in the water above the Isangila Fall.

From this point the river, though difficult in places, was quite passable for a distance of about 100 miles, as far as Manyanga, a native town close to the Ntombo Mataka Fall. Here Stanley began road-making again, past the long upper stretch of the Livingstone Falls, which had cost so many lives on his former voyage. It was tedious work; but another sixty miles of road took him above the Ntamo Fall, and soon his steamers were afloat in Stanley Pool. By April 1882 he had founded the station of Leopoldville, on the shore of Stanley Pool, and was on his way home for a few months' rest.

He soon returned to the Congo, and by the end of 1883 had founded two more stations, one at Stanley Falls and the other on the river Ruki. He had very little trouble with the natives, for they had learnt to respect him, and he now set to work to gain them over to friendship. By the summer of 1884 he had made treaties with more than four hundred chiefs, who, for a few pounds of beads, gave the society trading rights over their country worth millions of money.

After this he returned to Belgium; and early in 1885, by a treaty amongst the nations of Europe, the Congo Free State was founded and marked on the map of Africa. Thus most of the country, drained by 3000 miles of this mighty river, was thrown open to trade with the world.

Stanley was now hoping to spend a few years among white men, but it was not very long before he was called to Africa again. The Dervish revolt in Egypt had for a time swept away all the law and order that General Gordon had made in the Soudan after many years of labour. The brave hero, Gordon, had died a noble and lonely death at his post while trying to save the women and children of Khartoum from the murderous rebels. One of his lieutenants, Emin Pasha, whose real name was Dr. Schnitzler, was hard pressed in his province of Equatoria, and had not been heard of for years. Most people thought he was dead, till news came that he was still alive but in great danger, near the shore of Albert Nyanza.

The news made a great stir, and many people joined together to pay for an expedition to bring him relief. Stanley was made leader, and among the nine officers he chose to help him were two surgeons, Parke and Bonny, while Major Bartellot was second in command.

Stanley, as usual, gathered his followers from Zanzibar; and he made an agreement with Tippu Tib, who promised to find him plenty of bearers. Stanley had found

Tippu Tib untrustworthy before, and in trusting him again he made a mistake which helped to bring much trouble to the expedition.

In 1887 Stanley was once more at the mouth of the Congo; and by the month of June he had carried all his stores, by road and river, to a strong camp at Yambuya, on the Aruwimi, 96 miles above its junction with the Congo. Beyond Yambuya the bulk of their stores could go no farther, till 600 bearers could be found, and these Tippu Tib promised faithfully to send in nine days' time. Then Stanley, though twice over he had found Tippu to be faithless, left Major Bartellot and about 260 men, with most of the stores and ammunition, at Yambuya, to wait for Tippu's bearers, while he himself went forward with 389 men. The other white officers remaining with the rear column were Jameson, Ward, Troupe, and Bonny, the surgeon; while Stanley took Capt. Nelson, Lieut. Stairs, Jephson, and Surgeon Parke.

On June 28, 1877, the advance column left Yambuya to follow up the river Aruwimi, and its branch the Ituri, and then to strike across to Albert Nyanza. The distance, in a direct line, was about 380 miles, but the march was made longer by the winding course they had to take. They were in the middle of the great forest of Central Africa, which is 600 miles long and 500 miles wide, and they had to pioneer a path to its eastern edge. It was an unknown country to all of them, and through much of it they had to cut their way with axes and bill-hooks. So great were their hardships that the men began to break down with fever and fatigue.

On July 4th, as the river seemed passable, the pieces of their steel boat were screwed together and she was launched. Some of the sick and the loads taken from fifty bearers were put in her; and these men, with forty-four boat-bearers, were then able to help the others. They now began to collect canoes on the way, and by the end of the month their fleet numbered fifteen vessels.

At first the natives were unfriendly and often attacked them, shooting from behind cover with poisoned arrows. Some of the poison was made from dried red ants, another kind was prepared by boiling down a species of arum, and this was so deadly that the natives always made it in the woods far away from their villages. In a two days' skirmish, Stairs and nine men were wounded with this poison, and four of the men died. The natives also fixed sharp and poisoned wooden skewers in the tracks to their villages; and so cunningly were these hidden with leaves that even the wariest of the men were wounded in their naked feet.

About the middle of September they came into country desolated by Arab raiders in search of ivory and slaves. The forest was silent and deserted, the villages empty and ruined, the plantations wasted and over-grown. Here the horror of their journey began. For 197 miles, nearly a month's march, they lived mainly upon fungi, herbs and roots. This soon told terribly upon them, and the sick list daily increased. On October 6th the waters of the Ituri were found too wild for the canoes, and now they could not carry all their sick. Nelson and fifty-two men were left in a place afterwards called Starvation Camp, while the rest pushed on to an Arab settlement at Ipoto, supposed to be distant only three days' march; but they did not reach Ipoto till October 18th. While on the way they shot Stanley's donkey for food, the men almost fighting for its skin and hoofs.

Jephson at once hurried back to Starvation Camp with food, but he only found Nelson and five men, and two of the latter were dying. The survivors were almost skeletons. Stanley left all his sick with his boat and most of his stores at Ipoto under Nelson and Parke, while he himself pushed forward with a light caravan.

In November they were passing through Pigmy land, where the little dwarf natives ranged in height from 3 ft. to 4 ft. 6 in. There were two distinct races of them, the Wambutti and the Batwa. They were fierce little fighters and very clever hunters and fishers. They caught their game with pitfalls and snares, and were most skilful with the bow; even the wee pigmy children practised with tiny bows and blunted arrows. Food again grew scarce, and the caravan suffered much from hunger till, in the middle of November, they reached Borya's village in Ibwiri and found a land of plenty. After a short rest Stanley pushed on, and on November 30th came to open country after marching through forest for 156 days. The Albert Nyanza was now 126 miles distant, but, though he had to fight his way there among the natives, Stanley at last reached the lake near Kavalli's village on December 14th.

Letters had been sent from Zanzibar asking Emin to send his steamer from the end of the lake to look for Stanley. Nothing, however, could be heard of Emin, no canoe could be found, and the land march to the Pasha's province through hostile natives was impossible for Stanley's reduced band. Many men would have given up the search; but Stanley returned to Ibwiri, where food was plentiful and the natives friendly. Here he built a stockade, called Fort Bodo, and made plantations of corn and bananas, while Stairs went back to Ipoto for the men, boat, and stores they had left there.

On April 18th Stanley was again at Kavalli's with his boat, and he at once sent Jephson by water to Emin with letters. In eleven days Jephson returned with the Pasha, and the first object of the expedition was attained. Emin had been found safe and well; but now, when help had at last come, the Pasha could not make up his mind whether to return with Stanley or to stay in his province.

Stanley was by this time very anxious about his rear column, which Bartellot should have brought up long before had all things gone right. He therefore decided to go and meet it, and left Emin to go back to his province and make up his mind in the meanwhile.

Stanley hurried back with forced marches, but day after day passed without any sign or tidings of the missing column. He found his canoes again and went down the Aruwimi, until on August 17th he came to the stockaded village of Banalya and saw a white man among the crowd of black faces on the bank. On landing he found Surgeon Bonny, and soon learnt the history of the rear column.

Tippu Tib had been worse than faithless. He had taken gift after gift from Bartellot and made promise after promise; but in the end he sent just a handful of men, who not only tried to make Bartellot's men rebel, but also threatened the friendly natives till they refused to sell food to the camp, Bartellot could neither manage Tippu Tib, nor did he seem to know how to manage his men in the right way.

At last, on June 11, 1888, nearly a year after Stanley's departure, he started from Yambuya with all the men he could muster. He took half the stores forward a march at a time, and then sent back for the other half.

In this way he came to Banalya. On July 19th Bartellot and Bonny were the only white men at Banalya. Early in the morning a drum was beaten in the quarters of Tippu's men against Bartellot's orders. The major sent a messenger to put a stop to the noise; but the beating of the drum still went on, while shots were fired into the air in defiance. Bartellot went to enforce his commands with revolver in hand, and found the drummer was a woman. While he was telling her to stop he was shot dead from a loophole in the wall of a hut by her husband, Sanga, one of Tippu's men. Then there was a general stampede, in which they rushed to plunder the stores. Bonny came out of his hut and went bravely into the middle of the mob. One of Tippu's headmen with sixty others threatened him with their rifles. Yet, unarmed as he was, Bonny quelled them by his brave spirit and determined words. Then he got some faithful men together, and restoring order by degrees saved all the stores except 48 loads.

Three days later Jameson came up, and at once took Sanga to Tippu Tib at Stanley Falls, where the murderer was tried and shot for his crime. Not long after this Jameson took fever and died. Troupe had already gone home on sick leave, and Ward had been sent with a message to the coast. Thus the whole responsibility fell upon Bonny, and but for his pluck and coolness all Stanley's stores would have been shared by Tippu's men.

The Relief of Emin Pasha

On August 29th Stanley set out with a caravan of about four hundred and sixty people to cross the great forest for the third time. Some of the men were put into the canoes and paddled up the Aruwimi, while the rest marched along the bank. By the time they reached the Amiri Falls, on October 18th, Stanley had already lost forty-four men. Some of these had died of smallpox, but many had left camp without leave to raid food from the natives, and had been cut off and killed. Stanley also learnt on the way that ten of the deserters from Banalya had been eaten by natives.

Orders were now given to collect enough food for ten days' march, for there was little or nothing to be had in the country before them. Everybody set to work to gather plantains or bananas, which were peeled, sliced, and dried on wooden grids; and, when enough had been done, the march was continued.

The rainy season came on, and the toils of the journey were increased by the soaking bush, sticky mire, and swollen rivers. In one day the land party crossed thirty-two flooded streams. On October 27th they left their canoes hidden among bushes, and on the following day they came to Avatiko, where bananas grew in plenty. Here they caught two pigmies, a man and a girl, who were soon won over to friendship. Bonny measured the man carefully, and found him 4 feet in height, and 251 inches round the chest, while his foot was 61 inches long. The dwarf promised to guide them where food could be found, and, on November 1st, the caravan came to a banana grove at Andaki.

Two days were spent in drying more fruit, for no one knew when next they would chance upon food. On moving forward the undergrowth of the jungle was so thick that they took ten hours to cut five miles of pathway. Famine soon returned to them, and on November 6th fourteen men broke down with hunger. Next day Stanley sent Uledi with a large foraging party to scour the country in search of supplies; while 200 famished people waited their return to camp, with nothing to eat in the meanwhile but a little gruel of plantain flour.

In three days Uledi returned with food enough for several days, and then the caravan pushed on along the rivers Ihuro and Dui till they came to the banana groves of Indemau. Here they rested a week, while Bonny and sixty men made a wooden bridge eighty yards long over the Dui. For weeks their life seemed little else but famine and bananas by turns; and the state of famine and bananas seemed likely to go on.

On December 8th, thirty-five miles beyond the groves of Ngwetzé, they were in straits from hunger again. There seemed no reason for this; and Stanley, after a searching inquiry, found that nearly half of his followers had thrown their extra supplies away into the bush. The lazy rascals preferred the risk of death for themselves and the whole caravan rather than the trouble of carrying food. Stanley sent two hundred of them back to Ngwetzé to bring bananas, while he and the others waited at the camp they afterwards named Starvation Camp. The famished remnant kept up their spirits as best they could, for the foragers could easily be back on the fourth day, if not on the third; and then there would be fresh hope for the sick and the starving.

But the fourth day passed without the return of the rescue party. All this time Stanley had nothing to give the starving camp but a little broth each day made of equal parts of tinned butter and condensed milk with boiling water. The fifth day, and the sixth day too, were without relief for the sufferers, and Stanley began to fear that evil had befallen his absent men. On the seventh day he mustered seventy-six men who were still able to walk, and started to meet the missing party, or to learn what had happened to them.

They marched all that day, and lay on the ground all night, but few were able to sleep for the pangs of hunger. At dawn they struggled forward, and soon heard voices in the distance. Presently the foragers appeared with ample food for all, and Stanley found out the cause of their delay. Selfishly feasting in the midst of plenty, they had neglected their friends in Starvation Camp, whom they might have relieved in half the time. All returned to the camp that same day, and then the famished men knew what it was to feel thankful for food.

A few days afterwards, on December 20, Stanley reached Fort Bodo, and joined the party he had left there.

Three days later he pushed on to the Ituri River, and made a new camp at Kandokoré, where he left most of his stores and more than 100 sick men, under the charge of Lieutenant Stairs and Surgeon Parke. He himself went forward with the rest of his men to the Albert Nyanza, and encamped near Kavalli's, on a plateau 2000 feet above the lake. On January 16, just before reaching the lake, news came that Emin's Egyptian soldiery had rebelled, and had made both Emin and Jephson prisoners, intending to hand them over to the chief of the Dervishes, who was known as the Khalifa.

Stanley was prepared to rescue Emin by force, but Emin himself seemed quite unable to make up his own mind whether he really wanted to escape. He could hardly bear to give up the province over which he had been Governor for so many years; and he still hoped to bring his rebels to order and then beat off the Khalifa's attacks. Stanley saw that all this was hopeless, and he told Emin by letter to make up his mind in twenty days, or the relief caravan would start home without him. At last Emin decided to escape; and now came the question how was this to be done?

A new plot made by Emin's rebel officers settled the matter. They thought it would be very nice to get hold of all Stanley's rifles, ammunition, and stores; and in order to gain his goodwill they let the two prisoners go. Jephson reached Kavalli's on February 6, and soon told Stanley all that was going on. Emin followed eleven days later, and with him came some of his officers, whom he believed to be faithful. In reality this was a trick of the rebels to spy out Stanley's strength, and to tempt his men with bribes into rebellion.

Stanley saw there was danger in the place and determined to get away from it as soon as could be. Stairs and Parke brought the invalids and stores from Kandokoré, and on April 10 the homeward march to Zanzibar was begun. The caravan numbered nearly 1100, of whom about 600 were the faithful remnant of Emin's people.

At Mazamboni's village Stanley was struck down with a dangerous illness, which kept the caravan there for nearly a month. One of his followers, named Rehan, took this chance of deserting to the rebels with twenty-two men and some rifles. Stairs with forty riflemen at once gave chase, and in four days brought back most of the fugitives. Rehan, who had shot some of the friendly natives in his way, was tried by court-martial and hanged, and there was no more conspiracy after this.

On May 17 the caravan reached the river Semliki; but here the Awamba natives attacked them and refused to let them cross. Stanley sent several men to search for a canoe, and Uledi quickly found one tied to the opposite bank. Sharpshooters were now placed along the bank to keep the natives back, while Uledi and Saat Tato, Stanley's tracker, swam over the river. They managed to cut away the canoe without being seen; but after climbing on board, they were in full view of the enemy. The two men paddled for their lives, but the natives charged with a yell and showered arrows after them. Saat was struck in the back, but in spite of this the canoe was brought over in triumph. In a short while Bonny and five riflemen had gained a footing on the enemy's side of the river, and a few more canoe loads made them strong enough to drive the natives away.

Next day all were ferried safely across, and the caravan followed up the valley of the Semliki. On their left lay the range known to the ancients as the "Mountains of the Moon," whose highest peak, called Ruwenzori by the natives, rose 19,000 feet into the sky and glittered with sunlit snow. Stairs and a small party of men climbed 10,000 feet up its slope, sleeping one night on the way. Next day they were forced to turn back before reaching the snow-line, for their food was done, and the half-naked men were suffering from the bitter cold air.

On June 16 the caravan reached Russisse, and for the second time Stanley saw the Lake Muta Nzigé, from which the Semliki flows to the Albert Nyanza and thence to the Nile. He had now explored all the Nile sources; and passing round the east shore of the lake, whose name he changed to Albert Edward, he soon came to his former track. Once more he saw the hot springs of Mtagata, the hills of Karagwé, and the uplands of Usambiro. Once more, after fifteen years, the chiefs of Usukuma and Ugogo tried to extort tribute from him, though now they asked three hundred measures of cloth instead of the former fifteen. Once more he crossed the hills of Mpwapwa, the valley of the Mukondokwa, and the Makata swamp, though this time fortunately in the dry season. At last, on December 4, he reached Bagamoyo, and then his share of African travel was done.

As soon as he had finished up the affairs of the expedition, he started for England to enjoy a few years' rest after his long time of hardship and toil. In 1890 he married Miss Dorothy Tennant, who, like himself, was of Welsh descent. After the wedding service, which took place in Westminster Abbey, he laid a wreath on the tomb of David Livingstone, whose example and friendship had drawn Stanley to the career that brought him greatness and honour. For though Stanley's life was not so fully noble and heroic as that of the old pioneer, his work was none the less useful to mankind; for between them these two great explorers threw open the whole of Central Africa to the world, and it is now the duty of the nations who have shared the great continent to carry on the work of civilisation. We English, who hope for a great and lasting British Empire, have taken in charge the land belonging to nearly thirty millions of black men. All land, however,

RUWENZORI GLITTERED WITH SUNLIT SNOW.

is utterly worthless to an Empire without plenty of good, useful, and happy people to work upon it.

If we ever grow careless of the well-being of the natives, if we let them poison themselves with the abuse of rum, if we make them work for next to nothing while we get rich at their expense, then we shall bring both them and our Empire to ruin. But if we freely spend our money and knowledge in teaching them how to make the best use of their lives and to become active, healthy, and joyful in their own land, then there will be a grateful British Empire for our children's children. It was for this that Stanley worked, and for this he was made a knight in 1899, five years before his death on May 10, 1904.

9 781761 535567